Naked Letter

By China Muse

Copyright

China Muse

Naked Letter

system without express written permission from the author / publisher. Limit of Liability and Disclaimer of Warranty: The author / publisher has used its best efforts in preparing this book, and the information provided herein is provided "as is," and makes no representation or warranties with respect to the accuracy or completeness of the contents of this book and specifically disclaims any implied warranties of merchantability or fitness for any particular purpose and shall in no event be liable for any loss of profit or any other commercial damage, including but not limited to special, incidental, consequential, or other damages.

Dedicated to my wife Beixi whom I truly love for her inspiration, thoughts and trust. Without this...time here would not be.

Preface

Consequences of your action go pretty damn far.

Think now. While you can. It will start soon. You'll be distracted.

Remember. As if you can't forget. His sweaty face was greased-over, severely scared from acne. Rancid burnt meat, and beer jetted from his mouth. His breath poured into my eyes burning from the gas. He yelled something which I still have trouble understanding. Either I was to stop and drop my pants, or stop dropping my pants, or stop and drop the pants. How the hell could I do anything with his sizeable weight laying on me? Drop what? Do what? The yelling increased. His not entirely chewed food, splattering my glasses. His tobacco stained teeth almost mating with mine. I couldn't breathe. I was passing out when I felt the warmth of my own crap fill between my legs. My situation became clear after waking in foreign police detention.

That was a year ago. I think. I don't want to think. That is a problem for me. I chase my tail when thinking. Now, I spend the moments in staleness. Some moments have their own ones, but I try not to go in there either. I will always be that shy-fem. The others bitch of my poetic residence. When wanted, I was taken. Gruesome at first, but you learned there is no conservation in prison. I bled so much those early weeks I thought it not possible to live. Movements ratcheted pain along the spine through to the brain. When raped repeatedly, I simply passed out. At sixty-two years old I was considered fresh. It was not uncommon being anal rape and simultaneously give blow-jobs day and night. I learned I had to detach from the element to survive. Think of anything but the present action being preformed. Summer holidays. Signing lucrative business contracts. Getting drunk. Making money. Saving the world. Anything but salty cum sliding down your throat with three more cocks waiting in line, and one shoved up your ass. You were assaulted any time or place. For hours. No contest with guards or inmates existed.

I tried fighting at first. Protect myself, my honour. How they loved seeing you cornered, and squealing. Now I am addicted to the chase taking part in the rapes and taunting. There will be fun tonight and I can't wait till I fuck and drop dead exhausted. Do I love their tight holes, praying for their pathetic mothers rescue, forgiveness? I am that parody helping them pray. And they do scream their calls to God! Reflecting off rotting walls and ceilings, finally falling on to the floor, these dead hopes washed away with blooded water, flow down drains, collected in that transgressor of Elysian Fields, that abode of the blessed after death. Maybe it's been more than a year.

The Sift

'Conventional; last person in the world to commit crime; not very self-aware, and very compassionate; believes he is a very good example of what the best is'. My analyst remarked, two weeks before I left on a three week vacation, and it still rolls around. Before I left on holiday he released notes of our consultation to my ex-business partners saying to me, 'Done with the best intentions for your partners'. Into my fourth brandy on the flight for that country where Spanish is an official language, thinking if he'd been doing this all the time, forwarding private notes, what else was this dick fuck up to? Hostile takeovers, leveraged buyouts, and mega-mergers spawned a new breed of billionaire. In 1981 the average salary was $15,750. Life expectancy for male's 69.9, females 77.6, and minimum wage stood at $3.10.

BMW was $12,000, Mercedes 280 E costs $14,800, movies attendance was around 20 million each week, and the Equal Rights Amendment failed ratification. He actually convinced me of early retirement. It's now obvious the 'old partners' had their eyes' on several ventures. My company and its holdings for one. The adversary ex-wife second.

My daughter and three sons are far away. I have not heard from them in years. After the divorce they sided with their mother. Even thought they were in their mid-twenties, they acted as children. My fault as I spoiled them more than their mother. I gave them too much. Of everything. How that chock-chain would've soothed situations had I used it. On myself. I should have swayed long ago from the rafters in our barn, just above the horses. The scent of a sweaty horse. Nothing better than hunting with friends, in a company of dogs, and good bourbon. It brought out the animal in us. We'd enjoy brainstorming. Some of my friends were business partners my analyst shared details with. How I wish they were with me here. Prime bitch meat.

Not hanging myself after all the facts had reason attached in knowing it would happen regardless. Dislodged from that staid position of my mother I touched ground running. I looked back once when visiting the folks with my children. Sitting there watching senility form over my father thinking, 'Travel through the twentieth century. How I wish.' I saw my father at his end, shrivelled, sitting at the edge of the bed. My mother placed him in a facility and I never saw him after that. She was happy at last being rid of the man. I saw them kiss only twice. I learned to swear from their yelling tournaments. I learned my father had a taste of packing his bag and leaving for week-ends out of the house of, at one point, thirty-three cats and seven dogs, for his heaven. The beach. He openly gawked at women, shuffling around. A man in his late fifties, expressing his thirtyish. I did not to do the same. Yet, now with destiny crap hanging around, the thirty year-olds fuck my ass every day and night. Laying at night with an undefined release date, staring at the shit Mr Fat in the bunk above me, listening to moans, beatings, screams from other cells, and snoring from the other thirteen men in the cell, I ask myself one question; how could this shift in mentality take place so quickly?

Orange Teeth and Mr Fat

The under-cover cop whom I spat on for screaming, 'Vete a la Mierda Puta!' at me had orange teeth. The fetid sweat dripped off his face into my open gasping mouth. Pinned under the fat his landing on me, forced air to abandon my lungs as sperm leaves it's once owner in a screaming rush. He smiled feeling the oxygen leaving me, and then spat directly into my open mouth. Next, I heard voices beyond him, and then I defecated myself. I could not inhale, and in trying produced a low, whining sob. My ankles were grabbed, orange face rolled over and I was dragged feet first into a car. I lost consciousness as my head struck the underside of the half-opened door.

The lurid stench of my shit caused the brain to decide. Either play dead, or deal with this. But the eyes had another idea. If they don't focus on anything, they'll be just fine. But it was too late. An action dealt everything its own hand, as ice-water hit like stinging bees on your naked ass while humping in flowered fields. The oxygen burned, gulping I cried. In opening my eyes only the left shed information, sliced sense only a fraction. I raised my hands but only to the height of my abdomen, when the chains cut into the wrists. Again I cried. My mother came at that moment saying, 'If you don't stop I'll give you something to cry about!', when she would grab my hair and begin with the slapping. I'd try to pull her hands off but my hair yanked out. Moving away wasn't an option either, she'd often corner me. Afterwards, leaning-in as I cringed on the floor, she would whisper, 'Wait till he gets home'. My bladder would let loose. Just as it did now. Why would things change over the years?

There is a sharp series of slaps, then cries and further moaning. Those not used to it, troglodyte sex between men is not an event you want to observe often. I read what happened to German women when the Russian soldiers arrived in the remaining months of the Second World War their gang raping lasted weeks. The daughters too were not spared. Forced to watch their mothers sexually assaulted, and afterwards they were nailed alive to wooden crosses. The youngest women and children were often kept together in abandoned dormitories, schools, and then systematically raped with gruesome results. Here, new arrivals are treated similarly. Lasting upwards of several months until the next stumble along. Among the twenty thousand plus inmates, there are only a handful international offenders serving time. Authorities keep us apart. Startlingly I ran into a Norwegian man months ago for only a moment. Awaiting trial for embezzlement, he wanders the crowded halls. Pus infected skin pulling on his emaciated form. Muttering should I find some way, either through me or another, to have him killed. 'Been here six years. No visitors. No word.

It's the humane thing'. The crowd swallowed him. Taken toward that affliction. I haven't seen him since.

Tribulation in my own suffering is my own dealings. My right eye glued shut from the bleeding gash from my head having struck the car door, chained, whimpering, smelling my bowels, those conservative thoughts, beliefs held strong, ran for safety amongst that   stampeding logic. All fled leaving a seldom embryo. More cold water poured on me mixed fear with anger. Footsteps reached me, stopping on my right. Losing two teeth, right eye partially blind, numerous brandings, the tip of my right ear torn away by pliers or teeth, am not sure as the beatings lasted days. Two traded turns during the conception. One used a wooden staff, while the other a lighted cigar. They took me to 'the bed' consisting of a table. I was bent over, arms out to the corners, tied, and repeatedly raped by them and the staff. My impregnation began.

I did not shed a tear, and will never again. The fat fuck lying above me screwed my ass day and night for weeks went I first arrived. If you don't find protection when you enter this place, you'll be consumed. I became another bitch, and transport counsel (one drug is as good as another here) for an established 'leader', I explained to him my problem with Mr Fat. It was soon resolved. Mr Fat was tied down and I shoved a rusted nail having first been dipped in my shit, up his penis. He was left several days for the infection to get its hold. Six months latter Mr Fat still whimpers when he pisses. So do I care? About world events? My horses, the kids? Money? I have not seen anyone, legal representation or from an embassy, coming to the rescue here. I read an article year ago praising the person who can believe in the fact they are what they are and to live with that, enjoy that, love that. Sure. Spend some time here, cheer the person who believes. If you still are a person.

What possibly goes through the mind of someone boosting such recommendations? Where does their mind even come from? What form of hypocrisy are they born into? I washed my sins with charity. Contributing toward a number of causes I slept easy.

I did something. Not for myself so much, for the greater good as well did I thrive. Producing commodities the public required, even demanded for God sakes!! They bought hole hearteningly those blessed folks with their hard earnings, and I in-turn place their trust with actions for dead and dying in third-world countries. Marching yonder I believed none of it. Its pathetic infrastructure clearly out dated and single-minded. What good has any of it done? Why can't we simply just die normally? What's wrong with dripping shit? And by the Holy we want to give, indeed, and we must, but first a message from our diarrhea sponsors and their new treatment for that irritable bowel syndrome. The advertisement from my company illuminated.

The company had several products prompting fast, effect colon control. I targeted developing community's world-wide and awarded lucrative contracts. Did it reach the end-user? Indeed. Two present. I completed my contractual business as a provider. Distribution was not my matter. I enjoyed my wealth, my brainstorming. I handed new deals to fellow associates who were very thankful. We all sat around patting one an others soft assess. I was nearing sixty-two, contemplating opting out, confided with my therapist, listened to colleagues, and took long hot baths. Alone. Like it had been for the past twenty years. The ex was not interested in such lavation. I liked the bourbon, bubbles and masturbation for myself. She and I both on the way out, like our sex, mostly when we both had way too much to drink, in the dark, waking the next afternoon with a crushing hangover, a mouth tasting as if I'd chewed aluminium foil all night. I married at a weak point in life. At an end, sleeping in freezing rooms wearing two pairs of pants, three pairs of socks, and a cap, with a toilet whose water froze. No finances or none on the horizon. The only song I knew came when looking into the mirror, blood-shot eyes like a German road map, drivelling self-pity.

Mr Fat rolled on to his side. He whines in his sleep now. Does he pity? Maybe I should have shoved the nail in his ear?

Dozing off I thought very little of tomorrow. Fowl heavy odours, walls streaming with damp, fungus, rotting flesh (amazing how many different colours the skin alters), sex, maggot filled rice. A letter would come addressed too me. I wouldn't know that now. Now, I faded out. The letter was being read in the authority's office. Censored. I never received anything before. They wanted to know what this was all about. How could it happen? Who knew I was here? Who talked?

Naked Letter

Written Expression

It had been removed from its envelope. Smudges. The usual makes. Control lasts as long as power. Theirs existed in knowing or someone else they knew, of something. The seed is planted at the optimum time. The farm knows the harvest schedule. A child cries when the toy is lost. I am paid half of what I'm worth. I am not stupid. The have of the 'if' and 'what' of the all. How we give blood for that law. 'What had I've gone....?' 'Assuming that...' The rule of shoe falls near. They have a thickness that claps. The authorities sound shapes the iron doors holding us. Their shoe soles made not from rubber, have steel plates attached. Grotesque tap dancing shark fins, cutting through hallways of men.

It's worst if your dragged too them. Leaving your sanctuary, you know, won't be the same should you return. Might be you're looking through one eye instead of two. Have a partial foot. Half-a-hand. One functional kidney, the other sold. Domination.

Men here cry in spasms. Emotions excepted in small corners. Commotion ensues, disinterested sensibility gains root. We lose earthly elements, die lonely deaths shouting 'It's not my fault. I was tricked!' Among these cells, the only ambush is your stupidity. Here is real. Before here, fabrication and genocide of 'the truth' is the 'p' in piss. 'Things are just so damn boring'. 'I want to be important too'. 'The neighbours are lame. Let's eat 'em'. I believed I had all the answers, and a fallen angel. I had every right in screwing associates, reviling the ex's incompetent friends when visiting us, drinking till passing out. I had the colon cure after all, yet am the secret sabre rattler found over every hill. In groups I flourished. Alone, I wept and made sad, creepy noises. The ex-drove me to drink at times with her, 'Hey, go tell them they didn't pump enough shit out of the septic tank. I can't see the bottom!', 'They short-changed you five cents. Go over there now and get it back. Can't you be a man? Christ, I married my father!' I travelled extensively, away from her, her beating the dead horse attitude, into the arms of silence. Never bored with the angelic life I have, and I knew the neighbours were not lame, regardless her constant ranting's.

The handwritten letter on a single sheet denoted its feminine author:

I was sixteen when we first meet. You knew me as twenty-one. By now you will have forgotten us. It was warm that afternoon when you came looking for the room. I placed the advertisement hoping it would produce extra income. My mother passed away the year before. Leaving me. Lost. Indeed, the house, and I wanted it used for better purposes then the ones I grew up with, so I contacted the newspaper. You telephoned three days later. When you arrived you seemed, distracted. You lost in your own way. Are you still with that confusion? Our bewildered eyes looked the same, but you were quieter then. Still, you exercised such power over my shyness. You were surrounded by mystery. Authority. Fortune. And all those books you carried. I wondered what the man could be like with a backpack full. So learned. Yet, in all this, you were an ethereal child. I have loved you ever since and only wanted to go to you...

I have forgotten more then I will ever know. In reading the letter four more times, I still could not recall who she was. And when? It is a mistake. Gruesome humour. The authority's mental torture. A methodical reminder; better born dead then a life of uselessness. Placing the rolled letter inside my hallowed bed post wondering should the rain stop it would dry out some. I didn't feel the point thinking any more of the letter, anything but would entertain. I walked the halls, talked with others, wanting now only a great distance from the letter. I could feel the texture of the paper. Hear the crinkling sound made when holding it. My hands smelled of it. The words spiked, twisting into my brain. It's possessive. The paper had been poisoned. I am sure of it. Touching its vileness I contracted a toxin. It's eating my mind. I can't breathe!! Jesus I can't breathe!! Help me. I'm dying. I shitted myself. The grungy reek burns my eyes...It's running down my legs... Stop it, you're exaggerating. Take a breath. Jesus get a grip!! But these are something I've got to do. That compulsive feeling, belief, attitude that I'm important, but with lots of faults and weaknesses, which is easy to believe is being honest and realistic. My personality view. They were acquired after birth. Perception delivered. Leaning against damp walls, breathing slowed not wanting to faint, reaching down finding no foul mess between the legs, the thought came; the first thing I realized here, is I don't exist. What fragment of the mind orders this gaming? And why? What lessons to learn? While an accident, some walk away intact, others crushed. Random. Chosen.

That night I dreamt. It was raining. With considerable wind. I sat at a table looking out the window at a garage roof next door. Its gutter filled with grass in one place causing the water to flow over. It fell on a person holding an umbrella, dressed completely in yellow. I could not see the face for the rain was near horizontal from the growing wind. I was drinking tea. Movement on the left caught my attention. I turned. The person with the umbrella stood next to me. I heard its rasping breath. Ice formed on the tea cup. Droplets from the umbrella fell but did not strike the floor, pooling a foot above it. The persons shape was fine, thin. It did not move. The breathing slowed. Then stopped. I looked out the window and saw a woman standing before it, peering at the yellow shape next to me. Entirely wet she raised, pointed her open hand palm upwards toward the shape and spoke. I could not hear what she said; only watch her mouth open and close. She then blew into her hand as a lover blows a kiss, and the yellow form melted into the water that remained above the floor. The women outside lowered her head and walked away. Turning back I looked at the yellow water. It had frozen. I heard a crack coming from the ice. Then a loud snap. In the centre a small hole appeared. It grew several inches. And stopped. Scratching sounds came from the window. Looking I saw a person resembling a drawing of *Covetousness* I had seen years ago, tracing its finger on the glass. Whether male or female, I was not certain, only, it was half of both. I felt an itching on my inner-thigh. Whatever came out of the yellow hole was now twisting up my pants, almost reaching my genitals. I could feel consciousness returning. The dream was ending. Before however, I saw spikes thrusting along the growth through my pants, into my leg. The screaming woke everyone in the cell. Mr Fat wet himself.

Steal Away Their Brains

I was drunk when the other letter came. Same as the first. Single sheet. Similar markings. A couple of months from the first letter till now have passed. I hadn't thought much about it, or the dream that followed. Then all three hit. My brain curled in a ball and fell out on to the greasy hallway I wondered the days. Having visited with a 'friend' who made his own potato whiskey before receiving the letter. I thought it was the same letter and looked around for the theft who might be watching my reaction; he must have seen where I placed the first letter in my bed. I could not focus on the writing nor any face. I lay down, slept, and woke when my bed was knocked over from fighting.

I rolled around trying to stay out of the way. I saw the letter under one of the inmates who was being knifed in the eye by two others. Dark blood poured out, running down his face to the floor and on the letter. I thought it would be interesting while travelling to attend a local barbecue, of pig. I thought it would be very interesting to see how the pig was prepared. Slaughtered. The cries this man produced certainly came close to that of the pig. Fearful, shrill shrieking. Both pig and man knew their time was at an end. Both fought. The pig died quicker. The man took long minutes. It was intended.

Blood to sharks, is the same as fights in prison. Things rapidly become slanted. Reason becomes that of revenge for something that happened so very slight in detail. Someone gave you shit in the halls? Well, you went to work on them now. And if they were not in arms distance, then whatever was, sufficed. The means to vent. Anything to anyone. You became what you always hide. Beast. And you loved being free! In AA meetings I attended they often talk about the 'bad side' of alcohol. The animal of booze. I learned very quickly that if I don't let the animal feed, I would be its next meal. Here, keep them in a cage and once they're with liberties, they'll bath with what you ate last, wearing your stomach as a hat.

In a fraction it went that way. Instinct said play dead, but the dead here have been used for games and practice. The guy with the knife in his eyes rolled off the letter and tried to knee the other holding him. It didn't work so well. The one who stuck the knife in simply pushed it deeper. At that moment I grabbed the letter and crawled for the open cell door. Before I made it I was kicked in the chest, knocking the air out and throwing me onto my back. Cringing under the pain and loss of oxygen made me gasp, mouth working as the dead fish dies. I tucked my legs up tight. Someone fell over me, cracking his head on the floor, the blood splattering my face and open mouth. With that the air shot into me and I vomited. If I stayed in the confined cell I would be beaten to death. One hand holding my chest the other pulling at people who lay fighting, shitting, screaming also wanting to get out of there, I tried to crawl through. But we were being pushed back deeper into the cell as the halls filled with more inmates. More wars. Then the lights went out.

Solitary is like a closest where you can't stand or lay. Where you were let out, or not. Sometimes you stay there for days, weeks. Longer. I was there for what was said, eleven days. I didn't bother counting. You don't know day from night anyway, and the light shown through cracks in the door always stayed on. The authorities claimed it was I who started the riots nearly resulting in the entire prison population in that wing, of being burned alive. The prison had high ceilings. Attached to the ceiling are buckets of oil. If problems escalated the buckets were released falling onto the floor, and then ignited. An effective control method, seeing there was little to burn except people and fouled mattress.

I passed the time thinking. When returned I realized, I had gone quite mad. That some of my leaves had gone bitter. That I was able to stuff the letter into the crack of my ass before meeting the 'closet'. That after reading the letter several times I understood its origin. That staying alone grasping its contents showed me there is fate, and I wish I fucked around more in college. That maybe by fucking around more I would have a better insight in me, this world, and the one I just entered. That maybe karma is a joke. That there is no test after death. That maybe I am bisexual. That if I met my ex I would tell her watch out for the dead. That they will come for her. That I spoiled my children. That even my dog is spoiled. That friendship are deadening because they were a lie. That I feel the urge to knife someone, when I have it in my hand. That here I can knife someone for enjoyment. That here is real. That the second letter said:

You stole me. I know that is strange, but it's true. After I fell asleep, each night you would come in and steel a part of me. In the morning, I would wake with your scent on the pillow. Still lingering, faint, but there. Your side of the bed, still warm, carried the traces of our love making. You would always rise earlier then I. Sneak off for a walk, returning before I even realized it was still a dream. I dreamt of our passion. And I only have you left in this world. But you are sporting with things, and with men. What do you need in me? You don't know me, and I have never ceased loving you. Even when you left us. My limbs ached. A fever. I was caught by your infection, of my love which was once, yours. And the pain must be told. For because of this I am writing you, from this place which my heart has no concern. But of only for you... How passionately I remember every detail we had, as clear as it just passed. I realized very soon you are several people in one. That you look through a child's eyes; and at the same time you carry the weight of others which has made you callous. People see only one side and not the other. I grasp this secret on first glance. Completing your spell of attraction. In this world you were the only thing of interest. My life designed for yours. And you removed and compromised it.

Affectation

Throughout that dreadful solitary time, I waited. Then it seized me, so cold was it in the horrible darkness. Panic finds its home. Once in, not retreating, it burrowed. Hooking. Deeper. Cold wailing search the warmth. I knew who she was.

In1949 I took time to write my thesis along the Mediterranean. I stayed, travelling its coastline for six months, at camp grounds, abandoned farms, on the beach, and the occasional rented room. Knowing after submitting the paper I would have to find secure employment, this was to be my 'cogitates scheme' measure. I had money from my parents. Knew what I wanted. So simple. After three months writing and re-writing, travelling and drinking I needed to sleep for two years. There it was. The signal, 'Room to Rent'. Had I not needed the newspaper to cushion pointed objects in my backpack, I would have missed the advertisement.

Protected from the street with its cosy garden, the small house showed a note of sadness. Drooping eyed top room windows blanketed with old black curtains illustrated neglect, and loneliness. The front door painted deep bourbon sold me. The property closed-in with a frail wooden fence had certain charms drawing immediate attention towards its age. Certainly older then it neighbours, it stood with quietness that spoke a need for attention. Not spiritually at any sense touching the wooden pickets produced warmth. Late afternoon, the sun had been out all day, yet the sensation not from daylight, felt comparatively full of emotion. The warmth spread over me. A blanket with yourself. Then her voice came showing a time where I did not want to travel. I believed in what could be seen. Not phantoms within the weaker souls of men. Sprites in the night. Nor Christ turning water to drink. Who worships a figure, tortured gruesomely dying on a wooden cross, celebrate it, and then mischaracterizes people of different, or no faiths?

I did not want to love, or any part related too it. She was dressed simply. Straw hat and a shovel. The sun behind her, skin tired, she smiles. A young couple happily married. She became pregnant. Then his parents forced her to have an abortion and divorce their son. Because they felt he loved her more than them, and in old age he would not look out for them. That story came to mind as she walked across the small garden. Approaching the fence the breeze brought her scent, and with it never a divorce. And we would have twenty children. All happy. Forever. Love.

And I do, did, still, want, can't have her. I do need to stay insane. I can't stand upright. Laying horizontal could bring a climax. That passing out a blessing. Then I'd not remember her. And I forgot her. For years. How did she find me? If she found me then other has too!! They know where I am!! Saved. At last. Now I can be sober. Help those I didn't. Love as I didn't. Be a man. At last be a man. A whole man. Just what mummy and daddy wanted. They will be so proud!! Our brave son who became a man and did brave things. Brave sweet boy. We love you dearly. Yes.

Delectable a cockroach can be. How I love watching them scurry between my feet, crossing the toes. Considerable vitamins too, and what flavour. That essence. What gusto. Why if I could just package this it would make a fine retirement nest. Yes it would. Why people would line up craving the distinctive qualities. Demand would be great. I should plan well ahead. What of sustainability? True. That could be an issue. I could import. And export. For a while. But not strain the source like those fools and their potato chips. So over-abundant they haven't any taste. Salted cardboard. No. My treats will be sold exclusive and with a twist.

'What twist?'

I don't know yet.

'Well, why do you think it'll be better than chips?'

I know.

'Know what?'

Yea.

'What?'

What.

'Jesus! What is it that you know?'

About what?

'Listen you chicken dick fuck, screw me and I'll cut you sideways slow and deep.'

Chicken fuck?

'All right that's it.'

Wait you think I'm a chicken, or what, that I have sex with them.both maybe?

'You need to start thinking of her.'

Yes I do want that, but can't.

'Well, you should because this knife is going to slice off your forehead.'

But I told you I can't think of her. Please put that away. I'll be good I promise!!

'Fuck you, now hold still.'

Oh please wait, Christ that hurts!!! Wait for to be sure...it gets better cousin. Stop, oh God please stop I'll be a good!!!!!

The cell door opened, I fell out scaring my insect friends thinking why few scientists have tried to see whether bats have a discernible influence on insect populations. I tried opening my eyes but was blinded for sure from my missing forehead. Those bastards cutting me like so. I will find his mother before this is over. And I yelled that too. I think. I must have. Why would there be banging at the door from authorities telling me to shut up or suck dicks?

But I could feel the blinking of my eye lids. Tiny clicks. Click, click, and click. We are all so happy now. Click open, Click close. Oh happy, happy, joy, joy time. I'm not blind just in the dark.

'Con los palos.'

What do you mean 'with bats'?

'La recuerdas?'

Shut up, I'm asking you about bats and not about if I remember her.

'Ha mentido a su.'

Bull shit I did not lie to her, she knew about me.

'No todo.'

Yes, everything. Screw this I'm leaving!!

'Que la amas?'

What?

'Que la qusta?'

......

'Has oído hablar me hizo que la amas?'

Yes. Yes I loved her.

'Ir a su.'

From here...how the hell can I go to her?

'Come el murciélago.'

Eat the bat?

'Sí, está bien condimentado.'

The bat is well flavoured?

'Sí.'

Again, the door opened and I fell out thinking bats migrate there in the summer and are considered a major insect exterminator. Yes. I recalled wondering about these bats while curled on the floor. Then it became wet and warm, than bees started biting me. Were the bats bees now? And what is that loud grunting sound? Why is it so hard to breathe? And the smell of garlic all around? Barley perceptible, I come to bent over a table, one authority laying on me, shoved it in my ass, tasting salty, warm liquid squirting on my face and neck. The other, busy letting his piss-load into my gasping mouth, laughed.

Her hand reached opening the gate, allowing me entrance in a world where cats lazily lay on window sills, scented flowers drift in bed sheets, and my first orgasm from love ensued. She spoke of the room to let, its condition and should I be interested the availability for short and long term agreements. Nonsense. I heard only the lifting of her breasts, and whispers her thighs made as she walked toward the front door of the house. Her shape seen clearly through the light dress shocked me. She wore no bra, her firm nipples erect. Roundness of breasts, complimented her buttocks. She opened the door and turned, smiled slightly, seeing I noticed her in this way. She was used being looked upon. It didn't bother her and why should it. I often thought we should all be naked. As she passed through the door, I followed pressing my hands on her ass, feeling her panties, reaching through her arm, grasped her breasts, and softly liking her neck. Her back arched, she dropped the shovel and placed one hand on my waist, the other between my... 'This is the living'. She said softly. I had neither the courage nor imagination to do anything. Only dream of. That ultra-masculine ego, shadow of wanton respect, lust. Disguised.

'This is the living'. She said softly moving through the room towards the large front window. 'Sunny and fresh air', she spoke reaching up unlocking and opening the window, looking back at me, waiting for me. I could taste her, lifting the dress, pulling down her panties, kissing her wet, warmth deeply.

'The sun. It comes through half of the day. And very quiet here.' I felt my genitals warming, getting hard. She might see this. I moved toward the window and looked outside hoping to draw attention away from my growing erection. To draw attention to my growing erection. To draw her to my growing erection. My light tan coloured pants must now show dripping cum. She'd notice the darkness. My stain developing. Filling the front of me.

'A kitchen in the back and upstairs are three bedrooms. I use one. You can chose from the other two. If you are interested.' We stood close to one another. At the window. At that time. At least...last...close. Losing myself was easier than I thought, feeling its pull as I left the cliff, over the side.

Muttering I believe the house to be exactly what I was looking for, that I would stay a month, that the sun shone fine, that I wanted her now from behind while we both looked out the window, heat burning skin. Branding. Both moaning, she pushed her curved firm ass against me. Hard cock sliding soulfully homeward.

'One month would be fine. Would you like to see upstairs?', her breasts full with sweet honey rising as she spoke. Licked her lips the smile grew on her showing teeth made for biting. How I wanted her to eat me. Hard.

Animal hard. The tip of her tongue showing itself calling me. Then her scent came. Spice that pulled the brain as she turned away from the window toward the stairs leading up. I wish I was drinking. I'd drop in front of her, spread the thighs and lick till the moon wept. There is no greater drug then lust in any of its forms. My pants weren't stained, and as I crossed the room taking the stairs, I was not drinking only knowing at that time, I could never handle a woman as I dreamt of. I knew only the vaguest of these manners.

The month showed my hidden youth, before birth. We spent time together in many fashions, always in distance. The absence lifted life's shrouding, lying film placed there when born. I never spoke to another as I spoke with her. What was the point. You simply understood elements that won't be shared again, and shouldn't. We were the orange and its peel.

I wrote when possible. Often dozed in the sun, smelled her frequently and masturbated only twice that first night when she said the following day it wasn't necessary. She said hearing my whimpering orgasm, and thought it interesting, and would confront me in the morning to resolve the issue. She confessed this as we sat over coffee and fresh juice. I grew embarrassed. She assured me it was fine and I should come to her when the need of relief commanded. There was never a month such as that one in my life. Since then, I hated everything that was not in myself, and knew the remaining time spent as clouded torture. I closed that time long ago. Not wanting to remember, drinking from a golden flask, I my king, moved on.

'There ain't never no other month?...Christ ya deserve this.'

Shut up.

'Ya simple. Ya think the sun shines out yo ass.'

.....

'Ya can't play dump. Ya are, but ya don't do it well.'

.....

'Ya need a vacation.'

I am not talking with you.

'Where was it ya went that summer to expand ya thoughts...ya know.. that sunny place?'

Mary had a little lamb, a little lam...

'Nice ya hide her away. Do ya ex know?'

FUCK OFF YOU SHIT FUCKING BASTARD RAPE SONBITCH FUCKKKKKKK!!!

'Might have helped had she.'

Oh that's enough!! That's just far enough with your sickness.

'Maybe yo ex always knew...?'

You're sick. Not here. Sick, sick sick....

'The troops go marching, laa dee da'

What?

'Sure. If it wasn't for them troops then you'd be talkin' nother language.'

For fuck sakes....!!!

'They done sacrificed n died for ya. Ya know that. In them battles.'

.....

'Other folks too. Some burnt up good. Incinerated they said. Tortured.'

Shit.

'Yep. Kept in camps n raped. Whatever.'

That's nothing.

'Ya was there. Ya saw it funny boy.'

Wrong! You lie!!

'Nope. Am sure. Ah seen ya.'
LIE LIE LIE LIE!!!

'Or was it yo pappy?'
WHAT?!!!!

'Now Ah recall it was him. Scare over his left eye, sort of made it hang down. Droopy we called him.'

GUARD!!!!!GUARD!!!!!!!!!

'No he ain't no guard silly. He's evil.'

GUARD. OUT OUT OUT!!!!!

'Oh ya. He an evil piece of work yo pappy. Look right through ya. Took the light from yo eyes. Then snatch'em with that metal hook he carried.'

No no no no.....

"Seen him drag them children around hooked like a fish. He loved it ol'd Droopy. Loved it fine'

Pleeessse....

'Always with a sweet sorta smile having them dragged behind him the way he done. Peaceful look 'bout his face too. My how they did scream though. Lord. I'd pray they'd die quick just ta stop that yellin.'

Yell-down war hell ride!!!!

'Ya wish. But ya ain't crazy yet. No sir. Take more buddy time with that.'

KILLYOUKILLYOUKILLYOUIWILL!!!!

'Don't want listen no more? Tired? Sleep some. Mind, wake them on that other side this here door and skin ya good they do. Even might hook ya like yo pappy done. Sweet like.'

FUUUUUUUUUCK!!!!!!!

The cell door opened and I fell out onto the floor. They began.

Small in Stature

How I love when you wrote. Often your hair in twirls, fingers working magic on paper taking notes. Later I knew your hands would hold me, those fingers weaving my breasts and thighs toward passion I longed for but only knew with you. Would only want that. With only you. You were shy at first then once we talked did you then relax and find your way. We walked often, you saying it helped your thoughts, so we embraced this, our new world with courage and together wondered life's mysteries. You wanting children saying as you lay on my lap gazing on wistful clouds. Lust on your mind as you sought the warmth in us. That held us. Close with no bounds for glory that one true love has. As you spoke I dreamed of time only with you and knew my love was what I had waited for. You opened this. You were its caretaker. I trusted all with you. For me, it was all that was, and needed no after, as I followed you into worlds drawn not from here. When then did we move before? How instinctual we have lost this, forsake of holding what thought of as wealth, now only damns us. Where have we gone? Why does time hold us? How is our love taken from us that which we desperately wish to give, and then returned? Who has done this?

Three days after release from solitary I received this. It took another week to understand it. My eyes were light sensitive. Beaten, raped and starved, keep me alive is the simple fact in wondering how she found me. And what the hell does it all mean. And remembering times with her. And wanting those times. And wanting out of here. And wanting a new life. And wanting the past year forgotten. And wanting to torture those that crossed me, from birth. And wanting that to take years. And loving it. And loving myself in knowing what I really am. And bathing my soul in that lust of knowing. And seeing the sky...

The potato whiskey friend visited me with water what little food he smuggled out or didn't eat himself. Walking was not an option, I was certain I had internal bleeding. Any movement save the eye lids caused convulsions of pain. Three teeth were knocked out and four were loose. The top of my left eat was bitten off. What remained gave off a foul odour. I washed the infection. It still stank. I stank. Everything had the same stench of no hope. Slow pustule rot. But she found me. Saved from impalement.

Losing count of those recovery days showed the real side of this prison. You can't trust anyone. At all. Potato whiskey guy was fine when sober but when drinking he loved to play. Just getting back on my feet he fell onto the blanket next to me whispering, 'You got letter' late one evening, or morning, I don't what to recall which. Now what goes through the mind at this time is beyond what most people could possible understand or endure. I knew it would come to this and payment was due. I am small in stature, but good in business. He was big and did well in beating. Three men went for him once. He tore the throat out of the first, kick one in the balls hard enough so they popped; the third had his eyes pushed in till they seemed to come out his nose. No one played much with him after that. He is Ukrainian and here because he cooked and ate his girlfriend after she was caught in bed with another woman. Could be the combination of the two has a morbid impact on residents here.

'Yes, I received a letter.'

'You know who from?'

'Yes, I know.'

'Want more?'

'What?'

Naked Letter

'You want more?'

'Letters? You know.'

'I know.'

'Many letters?'

'Maybe.'

Fuck. Here it comes.

'How much?'

'You pay now?

'Maybe. How many letters are there?'

'You not dumb son-bitch. Two came when you locked away.'

Oh come on!!

'Who has them?'

'Friend.'

'What does your friend want for the letters?'

'He want talk.'

'About?'

'Money.'

'I talk with your friend and then get the letters. Right?'

'Maybe.'

Oh I've enough of this shit, am goin' break fingers in my ass hole if this dick doesn't clear up!!

'What do you mean he wants to talk about money?'

'You want letters? Yes or no?'

Just breathe. If you breathe you calm down. He's simphisticated, simple but yet sophisticated, with a message, and who can shove his dick in you causing permanent rupture.

'Yes.'

'Good boy. You wait. I back latter.'

And he slid away.

I listened thinking he would return. And realized I was delirious. That he was never there to begin. Phantom potato boozer, and the simpering twat.

A few days later I tried walking the halls. Movement should loosen up things. I made it a couple of steps. That was enough and fell against the wall where I slumped, waiting. A cut here would end it quick. Someone passing by. Flick. It would be done. Saved. Not to go further. At last. But I would miss her. True. I would. She would miss me too. Of course! That's right. Yes. Indeed. Fool. I'm a fool. She's so pure. I left her. The way I left her. God she'll kill me when we meet. Maybe she'll do it before. Yes. Before we meet. She might just wait and as I pass on way to see her, pop. Oh shit you've fuckin' lost it now. Over the edge. But it's possible. Get a grip man. Think all this through and drooling from the corner of my inflamed lips, potato whiskeys feet appeared next to mine. How strange. Why would his feet be here in this hall? And they're facing me. Toe to toe. Absurd. I am drunk. He gave me some of his potato crap, rotting my brain, now unable to ever storm again! I hate this. I hate me because basically I just let people walk all over me for no apparent reason other than my own bitch-made-ness. My only defence; financially rape the simpleton fucks. And the strong arms reached under my struggling to maintain an erected limp form, Carry Hawking me away.

It was dark and smelled wonderful. Spaghetti. Not able to see but that fragrance was better than well-washes pussy. And I'm starved! But there was something else. Tobacco. Cigar. Good cigar. And something in my hand. Paper. Thick paper. Probably folded. And...and...My head didn't hurt. I lifted my hand instinctively wanting to touch my ear. That source of so much pain, but there was a bandage. Which I followed. It crossed over my eyes. And to the other side of my head. The entire head was covered. I traced my face, resting my hand on the chest, and understood I was dead for these were not the rags I have worn for months. I feel nothing, and smell heaven. She must be nearby. Waiting for me. But what of these bastard bandages. A trick from The Higher one. Penance. She's cooking for me but I can't see her. Wait. Be still. Listen. I think I...

'Will you shut the fuck up?'

Jesus I almost peed!!

'Whaa..'

'Shut up. Fuck are you smart or what?'

.....

'You always talk to yourself.'

'M..nut..dead?'

Sigh.

'In a couple of days, maybe. You're all right for now.'

'Shee...'

Listen. You're drugged. We had to cut you ear off. The infection would have killed you.'

'Mu errr..'

'Just get some rest. Nok will help you. Eat. Talk later.'

'Wert nuen...'

'Give him some water and a little food but not much. And Nok, if someone comes kill them.'

The door opened. The door closed. He left. Me alone. With a Nok. What is a Nok? And my ear is gone? What the fuck does that mean?!!!! We cut your ear off...!!! That's enough of this. Smell or not, I'm....

'Zit still. You fuckin' baby.'

What? Is that Potato?

'Putoutu...'

'Ya, what you think. I be your angel now. Maybe good or bad angle.'

Potato is Nok? He has a name? He's and angle? Is Nok also her? Could I have three more wishes Genie?

Cotton and Chunks of Blood Everywhere

Can art teach? Can it help give a clearer account of the world? And besides suicide what other philosophical problems exist?

Nok said I was in and out for three days. That due to a fever I ranted and raved primarily of a women, time spent with her and lost. I remembered none of this but seeing as he could have read my letters maybe he knew more then I. My Host whom I still had no idea of maintained a fortress and well stock. I hadn't seen foods and tobacco in months, years such as what he cornered. He had my letters too. Ones I haven't read. But Nok had. He told me of places and moments only she and I had known. Why couldn't I've been content being an vegetable expert?

It was over a week taking short walks under the care of Nok for me to start losing the pains from solitary. The head still hurt but it was a small consultation for having survived, but to stand here and try to fix my life is just a big waste of time. We don't want our lives fixed. Nobody wants their problems solved. Their dramas, distractions, or stories resolved. Their shit cleaned up. What would they have left? Just the big scary anonymous. Members of simpleton fuck.

It was another four days when I met the Host, returning with Nok from hall walks he sat on the stool cleaning under his finger nails. He didn't look up when we came into the cell. Nok picked up another stool placed it directly in front of him and motioned me to sit. I studied the face and cloths. Body shape. Manners. Ten minutes passed and still he cleaned. His most interesting facet being the chameleon attributes he possessed. He looked so simple. You'd pass him and not think twice. His long hair and beard cover the face well. All very neutral. Had we meet? How then did he know me?

I shifted on the stool as my ass still hurt from the rapping. He stopped, folded his knife, placing it in his pocket, and spoke for several minutes without stopping, always looking downward. When finished Nok touch my shoulder, placing the other hand under my arm lifting me, meaning time to go and we walked the halls. Still in shock from his words I was very glad Nok was near to keep me from falling or being beaten as in the halls if you are timid you're meat.

I was very tired when we returned; fell asleep before laying down, with Nok sliding me into bed. I dreamt of dark, blackened skis. I was in a school. The buildings were in ruin. I searched a way out, seeing hills not far I wanted to reach. Each room I passed became empty the moment I crossed its doorway, leaving flashes of student ghosts and teachers. Books, projects, desks all from the 1920-30's shined for a moment, then gone. Walking into one room I stood waiting, listening. I felt pressure against my lower calf. Looking down it was the feral cat I had known with her we used to feed, rubbing its malformed face, a raspingly wheeze as he always had, the only sound heard, came from him when content. Thinking he might vanish too I reached to pet his thin head when he jumped more than ten feet onto the window sill. When I last saw him he was practically dead, even with our care. That can induce a good mood. Smiling he reached up unlatched and opened the window. It smelt like rain had just passed over. I moved toward the window. The cat jumped out. Almost next to the open air my foot caught and I couldn't move forward. I tried again. It could only happen here, when looking down I saw the reason why and started screaming.

It became hysteria when Nok slapped me and I woke. Before that he said I clawed at my leg, screeching to have it cut off, rolling on the floor. He said he tried to wake me but he'd had enough when I tried biting him. I sat rubbing where Nok struck me and wanting never to sleep again, with wisps of dream leaving, taking its hint.

I'd been rolling around, moaning for an hour till he'd had enough. When he shook my arm is the moment I lunged for him, mouth wide open wanting chunks of his neck. That lovely taste of blood draining on my face, down the chin. Wholesome. And if I didn't have that I would suck it from the rats. Or so that's how he told it. Nok said I became wild, that my eyes shone another part not there before. What part? What the hell was he talking about? It was just a dream. A bad dream, that's all I explained sitting up, rubbing my neck wondering what had come out of the dream, and if it was lose in this cell. With me. Trapped too.

Nonsense I reassured him, probably caused by weakness and slight fever. Is over, nothing to think more of. Now I had to get to work I said. Nok looked down, his frame crushing me, focusing deeply. Chosen well by my Host. There's more in some then you might think. Certain beings just have what it takes looking right through you noting the inner workings.

Nok brought me papers, pencil then stood back watching. Observing every move with responsibility. I knew as he did, if harm came to me in his company, he'd pay. His fault or not wouldn't be questioned. Action would be swift; the Host knows the *way*. The *way*? What for love or money is the *way* in this place?

I needed a plan. Life plan. A plan to escape. With the Host and Nok. Or so that became the demand. Or not. If not, then I would never read the letters he had, or read at all. He would pull out my eyes and then cut off my fingers. It wasn't clear if I was first to watch him start cutting, or have the eyes done. I got the gist, and didn't listen very well after the first minute. It was always the same. One holds power over another and sweet love comes forth.

Here the I didn't want to be a table slut, I needed those letters. Escape wasn't on the map, but if you need you play.

I wrote two names down and gave them to Nok. He looked them over folded the paper and walked out closing the cell behind, and locked it. And I thought only guards had keys. While putting the key into his pocket the other hand reached into his back pocket. Walking away he threw a folded, tanned paper through the bars landing a foot from me. This communication of discriminate pieces of factual information seemed appropriate for Nok making least communications in order not to have to disclose the entire truth because of the prolonged time of explaining the entire truth or possible bullshit thereof. Fact of life around him.

The head swam as I bent down picking it up. I probably would never recover fully. Always plagued with retarded ailment syndromes caused in part from alimony payments for the fucking you get for the fucking you got, as the bitch gets the house and you get the shity duplex. Fate, or difference in energies. It all comes up the same; the clever with least amount of soul wins. How easy it is to be evil.

Fumbling for the stool I sat waiting for that disappearance of those conscienceless stars. When the blinding subsided I partial opened the paper, seeing the handwriting, refolding it, placing it into my pocket. Cowardice. Always that. Behind big deals and decks steamed the ship. I was skilled to the level of being as good as currency. Now fear of what I had done writing those names, and her, melting together as the good drug does, and when the head is in a complete state of confusion and anger usually caused by another person. Me. Afraid and angry at my own ineptitude, out-of-practice-life, I tore open the letter proving I am a whole-ass of a man, committing one's self to seeing a task through. By any means. But how do you comprehend your own demise, your own unimportance in all that man created enormity, through all the marble crypts and stone bridges and incinerators that lead to the market place? That immense ego of folk, believing the world will end with your death, is perhaps more rutted then life anywhere else in the city.

Dear, I believe you meant well. Your love was what you knew. It shaped you. From when you became first aware of it, it held you close. It never cheated you and always told the truth. You cherished one another in folds of blameless lust. Not questioning you felt at easy. So, you moved through life with the care of a traveller knowing your path. It was the grandest of moments for you both. Then we met. And you changed. Or rather your loved changed. It became aware of me, grew solemn. Defensive. It had no idea of how to share. It never had done so before. We became its enemy. And it smothered. The weight of age, time and want of others grew stronger within this love, so you abandoned me. To save us? Was that it dear? Was your thought to free us both so you sacrificed your love? Had you gone to that place where such deals are made? I know I loved you with all things. With all energies and meanings. I saw through life and knew this was caused by you. I could. Live. And learn love. Because of you my dearest. You turned, leaving, caring now a deprived existence. Of me. I too stopped. How could one enjoy after you? You dear always, always would be my joy. And you have gone leaving behind that shell which you first knew as that child. But there was a part I could not tell you. Till now. In not wanting your pain, I kept it close. I knew you would return, in fearing this I neglected life. I became finished with what it had to offer. Till our sons were grown could I then tell you dear. Of how you changed the scent of my world. Of your leaving, and what remained of this world. Of your bringing life to me, your departed spirit returning in the twins. So, dear. Again, you leave me and still stay.

I remember laying down after having read that. I wanted to forget what I had just felt. I must have dozed off. Deeply in fact. When I woke it was dark. There was something imitatively felt. In the cell I was not alone. It was not moving but I knew it was there. And very near. I could smell it. Sweet, musty. Blood smell. Laying still, it could not know I was awake. But it did know I was awake and I knew it knew. My brain gave in. Sending signals I'm going to die, drawing whatever it was closer. It now hovered over me, the stench growing stronger. I felt it. Please I have to live! I have two sons that need me. For the love of...!!!

Something touched my face. What was that? Who are you?!! It touched again and ran along my check down towards my uneaten ear. Fucking shit!!!! it was cold, thick, slow moving. It would take a year to reach the bed, and I am certainly not going to wait. Brain said to hands, 'Let's move Goddamn you!!' but too late. A hand grips my shoulder knowing my minds act was to flee, disappear into whatever, whenever. I rabbited on, thinking thoughts of glee, sunshine, non-conformist sex, booze, big ass tits with great hard nipples, money, lots of that, sky diving, fucking up the ass, being fucked up the ass, wanting to be fucked up the ass, fucking an animal up the ass, fucking animal up my ass, fuck wont some cock fuck my mouth!! fucking anything not to think of this fucking shit!!! FUCKKKKKKK!!!!

It kissed me. On the lips hard it's kissing me. That wet musty, sweet stank everywhere. Now on my lips. CHRIST!!! And its staying there. It's not leaving. Just fat lips. Stinking shit lips of some fat fuck I'll fuck latter. Oh yes I'll fuck you with rusted iron bars! Fuck I hate this shit! If there's tongue I'll bite it off. Cock sucking dick fuck. Yea give me tongue bitch! Oh yea. Do it now! Your sweet wetness I want. I'm going to open wide and you're going to shove it deep in my wanting hole you slovenly, dirty bitch. Umm yea!!! Happy times again. Excited thinking of this erotic stink-fuck scene about to happen in the dark I started getting hard. My cock stretched wanting free. Pants to confining. Reach down and grab hard. Please....

The lights came on and the lips left mine. But the hand remained that being well as I'd have fallen off the bed screaming, aiming for the nearest corner. What hit thy eyes with light and thou shall see. But God did not make things which stood over me dripping saliva and darkness onto my face. Nope. This was not that creation. It was made entirely from this place.

In focusing lay two options; wait, or fight. It was considerably larger then I. Fighting would be difficult, and considerably painful. The answer revealed itself through that pause, those few moment deliberating which action proved best. As the face grew distant, retreating from me I concentrated on it. Covered with some dark, now in areas drying fluid, it became morbidly apparent Nok had been loosened. And returned home with a prize. A modern day vampire gargoyle sanding almost erect, watching my every move, no doubt feeling my fucking thoughts too. Jesus what was this? Returning from a war against a greater army. Single battle with the minions. If I'd not know his shape, then I would not know him at all. It is just that. You witness events, yet the mind cancels their ticket. No see, no harm. There were chunks of blood everywhere. The side of his face. Neck. Back of his hands. Shoes. Shirt. All carrying someone who once breathed. Looking him over I thought how odd the size of his ears have become. Cauliflower shaped. And that look. That way he had when there, but not. Dislocated. Then the light fell away, replaced by a gentler one. The cell now had its own life. And the Host slide past Nok coming directly towards me. So swift he took the back of my neck in his one hand, the other gripping my wind pipe. Then the nails started digging their way in.

Instinctively moving backwards I felt Nok's bulk against me. The Host new this and tightened. Coming closer whispering into my gaping mouth, 'Done well Mr Bank. Now. Let's see if we can exhibit that same sort of enthusiasm. Who's the richest of them all?'

I raised my hand against his. I wasn't having fun without enough air. Nok grasped them, yanking both to my sided, squeezing his arms together; choking what remaining oxygen there was out. Giant pinch. Grandmother to her grandson's cheek. Touching.

'Mr Bank. Try harder.'

My mouth worked but only farts came from my ass.

'Now Mr Bank. That's not exactly what I wish to hear from you.'

More moth work. No gas.

'What's that you say? I'm the richest? Well indeed Mr Bank you are very correct. That also makes me the most influential. Wouldn't you say Nok?'

'Yes', simple enough reply from Mr Nok I thought. Still I'm losing clarity. Without that air stuff things get fuzzy.

"Would you agree Mr Bank? You don't mind me calling you Mr Bank do you, seems poetic knowing your past endeavours and such?'

Blacking out when he let go I dropped like all good stones do. Flapping on the floor wanting as much air as possible but finding little, the Host whispered into my eaten ear, 'Do try get your rest. Nok will see to your needs'. And floated off. Christ there are real monsters.

It took time to gather my brain. I sat up resting forward both hands on the floor, fingers curled under. I wasn't thinking. It is after all a painful fist lesson here, that should you fall, never, under any circumstance, ever curl your fingers. It is the easiest way to have them crushed. Nok just did that. One foot on the left hand with his weight was enough for me to pass out waking later that night in that place you never mention at funerals. Hell.

As he looked down wondering if I was human, I saw why his ears looked malformed. They were stuffed with cotton. He still hadn't cleaned off the chucks of blood and flesh. I looked away. For her.

Disinterred

Only the innocent are healthy. It's reasonably true everyone is corrupted. Everyone is sick. The innocent a vanishing breed, as nearly all of humanity is dead. Waiting to be exhumed.

This place ranks the best of planted seeds on bad ground. Your life worth little here, and what life before, is worthless now.

But I have a plan. The Host and Nok will love me for this. Short and sharp sort of plan. And her. If not for her I would have no plan for she gave it.

While nursing cracked fingers, now set somewhat straight by Nok, thinking of her and my sons the thought came. The Host said if I'd not produce then I'd be given. Alive. To the Warns.

Something had to give and she did. We spent time on the riverside, laying under shadows, legs in cool water, playing with our bodies. That first kiss of her soft tongue, sweet, merciful. Her scent triggered a stiffer erection, wanting her damp warmth, which she did not give for several weeks. Being shy she held herself correct, yearning what most others wanted or already had, but also her spirit not found easily, anywhere. I hadn't in anyway seen anything, like her before. Nor since.

One among hundreds; one adventure after another. Our time together, so being linked in that endless chain. Before then we knew disparagingly what life could be. Alien. Without ground. Frenzied. Of all those turns and stops. Waits and want nots. Should one fraction be altered we would not have met. Writing for the Host is not easy. He requires a sound business plan after leaving here. One not questioned with able resources. Now the brain splits in two with her and Him. If Nok appeared here I would lose all scenes, there is only enough room for the three of us presently.

As I work with Him I am drawn more to her. Our sons. That time and where to start now? What are their names? Are they feminine in nature? Jesus what is that from? Just a thought. Look at this place. You know what goes through the minds around here. Yes I do. Yes, and memories. Vague memories all dim and confused, like the glimmering, shapeless view of a stone in the bed of a swiftly running creek. Shadows chasing one another across my mind, but would not fuse into any picture. Strings of memory in the realm of feeling, and still I could not remember, truly who she was. It seems I must have dreamed of all these figures, must have dreamed often and vividly. And yet they had only been the phantoms of a dream. But true. The letters are real. Substance.

With the only good hand present, it needed a dream. The other with its fingers splinted   made for a holiday and wouldn't be back any time soon. Given the pain it's fortunate I had drugs. And these were good. Just one and you're off for half the day. My imagination took hold leaving that shell scribbling notes, plans. Drawings. My God I'm writing an epic! When things quieted down it wasn't nearly that. At all. It seemed though. If I only had some paint! What I'd give for a little god damn bastard paint!! You weren't able to think very well while on these. You simply lost track of time, only when coming down did you feel tick tock rearing. Pass the time. You would do just anything for that. It's always deleting my definitions. Paint. Fuck it.

The memories interrupting thoughts affecting my present. How can you think when most of it is governed by past recognitions? Hell with this. I need a plan and quick or Nok is on. He and the Host set me up the cunts. I gave them the names of two lousy shits whom the Host needed for examples. Fact one, these two where low-level bankers in a drugs cartel. They each had three years to finish. Then outward. Host saw them as threats. The way I worded it saw them as threats. Fact two, they couldn't find their own ball bag. They were just that. Dirt, shit, scum, unable to do fractions. Fact three, my giving the names branded me snitch. Fact four, I thought Host and Nok wouldn't announce how they got the names. Fact five, I was wrong.

I outlined to Host potential risks. And he wanted names. No harm giving something. Turns out Host already decided who and when. How was up to Nok who torn them apart, partially with his teeth though primarily using the hands and his patented razor rope. He claims it's his invention, an extremely sharp, thin wire that cuts incredibility deep and quick. Seeing it only once I believe it inflicts nasty, fabulous wounds. Nok told me he carries it hidden in his belt. What one can achieve when locked away.

Now the population here knows what I did. The Host showed retribution being served with the shoe-to-hand dance. And I will never be able to walk alone in the halls. That extreme, vile, personified bastard Host knew all alone, and spiking me in the dick hole good kept me breathing His dark, stale air. Either I'm with Him or the Warns start their feasting. But I want to be with her. I want the letters. I want out. I want to live long enough to be a problem for my children. I want to be rich again. I want the Host as my bitch just as the entire population is of this government. Nok told me there were two letters, that I could have one if the business plane was flawless. Jesus. What the hell does that mean? If I'd a flawless plan would I give it to you? Would I be in this shit if I'd a flawless plan? FLAWLESS PLAN? You stupid naked brain dead fuck. Christ I'm sick of all the totally mindless want-to-be's, non-lateral thinkers of, 'Oh hello I'm Mr Flawless, please have a seat while I skin you alive starting from the legs up'. If you shoot me will it hurt? Much? Now that's thinking for this group.

The drug marched on, the brain loved that, and the and I doodled freely. The papers filled with warm crafted ideas, none linking with anything important, except with the hours passing. The paper slipped and dropped on the floor. And spun so I was looking at what I had drawn, but upside down. In that moment I noticed something different in the lines and dribble I played with. The thought came; hours passing. Passing hours. Passing.

Reverse that. And expand. Interesting. Yes, it might just work. Lovely. That world of uncertainty, anchorage for myths of metal afflictions.

Last Two

I spent the remaining day and night going over the details before saying anything. Nok brought food, I kept busy making notes. A happy couple. The plan emphasised decision-making tools. No fixed content for it. Rather the content and format is determined by the goals and audience. It represents all aspects of Host's business planning process declaring vision and strategy. Host told me very little of internal works, only his 'idea' formed with 'make it happen' attached. Therefore, I placed sub-plans alongside to cover finance, marketing, operations, human resources (it could apply) as well as a legal plan, when required, if any, yet most likely not.

At first not even articulated. Held numbly, conscious of only having an idea. Then reaction settled in. It had a great many risks, almost too many to depend on it. It was a process which developed in my mind along odd routes, directed, fruiting when necessary. Whatever straitjacket had been about me sloughed off. It seemed both brilliant and impractical at the same instant. The complexity toward it made me excited and troubled, close to laughter. There was only the necessity and one's own reactions to it, concluded in its final analysis.

Nok uses kinetic energy. It needs release. Host works with this exceptionally. Nok loved him, as both gained varying capacities. Being only required for a moment in their environment had its source. I realized that when Nok returned with cotton shoved deep so not to lose concentration. Sharp, sudden noises bothered him he admitted. A great deal. Cotton reduced their screams in his brain while he worked. His focus intense, competing with a fierce purpose. Art created is not natural. Nok is a masterpiece of walking artwork; accomplishment from another place. His study of pain anatomy mastered, applied with care in knowing most deserved this attention, smile saying, 'When lovers fade, they walk through that search of earth'. If ever torn apart, I'd want him for that.

When it was quit latter that night the Host appeared. I wasn't sleeping and watched his manners opening the cell door. So feminine, his dark evil princess shadow drifted toward me. Then stopped. 'I understand you have something of mine,' speaking openly unconcerned with residents, the tone sharp with business intent. My testicals chilled. 'Yes.' I am not for sale. I sell, but not myself. That's what I wanted to say, instead I grunted something which irritated him as he couldn't understand the contracted bowels I experienced and thought I lost my bearings. I knew this. At the moment I grunted he was upon me and I felt the blade under my left eye applying discomforting pressure. In a moment it would either pop my eye out or start slicing. 'Well...?' breathing up my nose, amplifying his garlic, alcohol reek. His weight shifted more onto my chest causing the knife to move slightly downward and out towards my ear. He felt my stiffening.

Not wishing to move, knowing he'd push the knife deeper, I slowly breathed out, 'It's not written.' He smiled. I felt the skin tightening on my back. 'And it's complicated.' His lips became horizontal, stiffly whispering, 'Let's make it like bread then.'

In his eyes bread's attuned with family traits describing wholesomeness, simple. I spoke slow and deliberate, always watching his eyes. They never left mine. It was his manner. The right he had of seeing your own self. Seemed born with it Nok said; as long as he'd know the Host he'd always have this infliction, this disturbance, allowing none the grace of escaping his presence. You became drawn toward him. Seductive sadism. Love attached. You wanted to be there. With him. He took you away and gave you, carried for you, cherished you. You were in His light. Stupefied. Caught in a group with other clowns to short of a circus, you gave in.

His thoughts shifted, the slight movement in his eyes gave Him away. I stopped wondering, it became clear. He didn't think much of the plan. I felt a grip on my shoulder. Nok forced me deeper into the mattress. The knife left my throat. He stood, walked over to the chair and sat down. His back to the bars I couldn't see the face, only His hand moving across the side of the neck. Comprehending He stayed there. Nok stood back sitting next to him. That's the last I remember of the two. When I woke they were gone. Next to me lay one sheets of paper. Sticking the match the candle was just enough light...

We are waiting for your return. The boys are thrilled knowing you are near the end there. Your new life starts here dear, with us. How I have wanted you close. The years gone, wasted. But now dear we are soon lying together. As we lay before your soft touch and lips upon me. How I become lost thinking of your wanting me. How I wanted your love deep in me. How the orgasms pulled us into that deeper sea. Oh how our first love on the beach that night...it was cold but we both knew it could harm only the naked skin. We both took great care and time as the water rose and took us. I was only with one other man before. With you I had forgotten all that of before. I hadn't loved, lived till you....oh dear think of those times again I will certainly die. A wanted death...and you will be here soon...saving us all. You won't leave us will you dear? As you left me before? You won't leave the children too? Oh dear after you I only wanted it to end. The mind wanted you and the body had to have you. But you were gone. And you never contacted me after. Can you understand what this means? You left and that was all. I had no idea what had happened. What was it I had done wrong? And you never gave me the address of where you are. You promised before you left but when I woke you were gone. And what you took in your leaving...I became damned.

Then learning I was pregnant I couldn't stand it anymore. They would always remind me of you. I learned to hate what was in me. In time I found a way. To heal...to love our children. I sold and moved from the house to the large city, renting a small apartment, there giving birth. There they grew. There gossip wouldn't harm them as it would in the house. Family with no husband, nor father. Scandal. There they are at school, and there I teach. Living as best we could. Some neighbours have well intentions, other not. I have a very good friend who knows the story well of us. She can't have children and her husband left her. She is often here helping with the boys, in the early days I bless her for without that care she gave, I would not be writing this letter. But you are soon here, back with us...my love, so dear, my strength is in you. We wait.....

Waiting for me. How does she know all of this? Before the answer came Nok opened the cell door, in two steps he was beside the bed with one hand on my neck spoke softly, 'Any word and I break it. Walk.' The letter fell onto the floor, and into the halls we moved quickly as morning arrived with men walked about. Nok with one and under my arm firmly guided me. At a moment we suddenly turned into a hall I hadn't been before with three guards standing next to a door. It was opened and we walked through and met the man who arrested me, with two other men also not in uniforms. He sat there smiling. Waving his hand, an inner door opened, and we walked down a dimly light hall that twisted then stopped. There was no point asking Nok what this meant. I stood there with him, waiting. A loud click heard through the wall where we were standing, Nok pushed which swing open the hidden door into a room with a chair, table, and the Host standing in the corner.

There was one light directly over the table and chair, Nok moved me into the chair, closed the door, and waited. The Host only looked at the ground, while speaking. 'I have the last letter for you. I know you want it. Before I and Nok leave this place, because you have been so helpful I give you the letter now.'

Yes dear how could I know? Where you are, when you will be here with us. I had to search. But what does it matter. You are safe and you both will be together that's what I live for, rather lived for. You see I am the neighbour and author of all these letters. My dear friend whom you abandoned died last year. Not wanting to live without you and not wanting them to suffer either she took your children too. She spoke of you often, then seldom, till nothing. The pain of it was more than could be born. As they came to collect their bodies I knew you had to be found. Mr Host has been kind enough in forwarding these letters, and I must thank him in taking such good care of you. The arresting officer, Nok and several others will benefit from the wealth you have no longer access to, or need of. Some time ago your holdings were transferred, and the account closed. My only wish, I was there to watch and participate. I understand Mr Nok is very good. Do enjoy these moment dear. Just as you did before you left them in near starvation of broken minds. Yes dear I so want to be there, but Mr Host inform me it will take considerable time, extremely slow I believe he mentioned. It seems dear your plan for him you carefully made would have lead him into great trouble. It appears he is not very happy with this. Well dear, they are waiting for you. She will have much to say too I am sure. As Ms Nok needs to relax, he'll take great care with you.

The paper drifted to the floor. After tightening the leather straps around the wrist and ankles Nok stood in front of me pushing cotton deeply into his ears. The Host raised his head looking at me as Nok pulled out his patented rope.

His End

Naked Letter

Made in the USA
San Bernardino, CA
04 March 2017